EVYN HUNTER VERSUS THE ZOMBIE CURSE

EVYNHUNTER VERSUS THE ZOMBIE CURSE

PATRICK NIGHT

Evyn Hunter versus the Zombie Curse

Copyright © 2015 Patrick Night.

This is a work of fiction. All of the characters, names, incidents, organizations, and dialogue in this novel are either the products of the author's imagination or are used fictitiously.

iUniverse books may be ordered through booksellers or by contacting:

iUniverse
1663 Liberty Drive
Bloomington, IN 47403
www.iuniverse.com
1-800-Authors (1-800-288-4677)

ISBN: 978-1-4917-5043-8 (sc)
ISBN: 978-1-4917-5042-1 (e)

Library of Congress Control Number: 2014920991

Print information available on the last page.

iUniverse rev. date: 5/5/2015

CONTENTS

PROLOGUE

1700s—SOMEWHERE IN THE CARIBBEAN

A lonely skiff slowly slides out over the calm water of Midnight Bay. A lone hooded figure pilots the small boat as it cuts quietly across the Caribbean inlet. The water shines brightly; the mirrorlike surface reflects the stars, and the light of the moon casts shadows across the water, keeping the drifting thief hidden in the night.

Looming up ahead in the bay is a large sinister ship. Its dark sails are strung up, and its anchor is down at the bottom of the black water. Intricate designs elegantly line the hull of the large boat; the figure of a beautiful mermaid appears as the small boat rounds the front of the ship.

The small craft slowly approaches, and the man very cautiously pulls up alongside the ship, trying not to make any unwanted noise. He pauses for a moment and listens carefully to the unexpected silence of the large ship. He swiftly climbs the anchor's immense rope line, hoping not to attract any attention, and then secretly boards the quiet deck of the pirate vessel.

The thief steps softly onboard, and instead of the ocean filth and damage he'd expected to find, he discovers that the ship is exceptionally clean. Freshly stained wood gleams with rich lacquer. Intricately painted and carved wooden railings and ornamental brass fixtures surround the clean wooden deck. Colors that looked dull in the night, upon closer inspection, are brought to life in an imperial and elegant way. The dark sails now look rich with deep vibrant colors.

This ship has never seen battle on the open seas. To any unsuspecting passerby, it is not a pirate ship at all; but rather, it would appear to be either a government vessel or one owned by a rich statesman. The shadowy thief knows for certain who captains this ship.

There are no loud pirates or sailors onboard; they have most likely taken leave to enjoy the pubs and saloons of the port town. Also, there are no rude prisoners stowed away in the brig below to make all sorts of ungodly racket.

There is not a sound onboard as the hooded man carefully makes his way across the tidy wooden deck toward the captain's quarters. He pauses for a moment with his back against the cabin doors, curiously listening to the silence.

Still, as the hooded thief enters the captain's personal quarters, he has the lingering suspicion he is not alone. He knows there is always one man who stays on the ship: its captain.

The shadowy figure had once been the captain's first mate, and he knows his old master all too well. The thief has boarded the ship to steal the captain's most precious item: The secret key to immortality, the magic to create and control undead servants. He has come to steal the captain's personal journal, which contains the description of the arcane ritual. This betrayed first mate, for a long time, has sought the power to link the undead to himself as their creator.

The manner in which the man searches the captain's cabin is most intrusive. Looking through books, along shelves and tables, and inside boxes, chests, and drawers, he finally discovers what he has been searching for.

Right out in the open on the captain's bed, for anyone to see, rests a book. It is a small journal, bound in old leather and accompanied by a small vial of red liquid strapped to the book with a piece of ribbon.

As the thief closely examines the red liquid, he is alerted by a voice from behind him, a calm voice, thick with a deep French accent. Turning to greet his old master, he secretly pockets the journal and the vial.

The captain steps into the dim cabin. His clean, tanned skin and stately clothes set him apart from the ordinary hatchet-faced pirate captains. He wears expensive jewelry, the finest leathers, and intricate fabrics that are colorful and finely tailored. "It will do you no good. Only pain and misery will come from you abusing the gift." The captain speaks with the tone of a concerned father to a wayward son.

The young apprentice says, "This gift that you hold so dear? This curse which you refuse to share but have selfishly bestowed upon me?"

"It is not for you to wield such power. It is a blessing in the right hands, a blessing that I have given you."

"You have cursed me! You selfishly hold the power to enslave, to raise an army, and to govern over entire nations if you wanted!"

"It holds the power to save lives—to save the ones you love from death—and to respect life. You know not what you do—"

"We shall see, old friend. From now on, the power will rest in my hands." And just as quickly and quietly as he invaded the ship, like a shadow lingering over the dark water, the thief is gone.

CHAPTER 1

HIGH SCHOOL

Evyn Hunter stands alone on the corner of King Street and Main Street. His short blond hair wafts off his forehead in the slight breeze which is blowing down the empty Newport city street. His blue eyes squint in the bright California sun as he looks around.

The corner of King and Main is usually the busiest and most central intersection in Newport. From the intersection, he can see all the way up and down Main Street. Lined with nice sidewalks and old-style streetlights, it's full of shops and businesses, small cafes, restaurant patios, and elegant, welcoming front entranceways.

Some shops have large bay windows displaying their newest merchandise, and others have big signs and flowers that make the street pleasant and welcoming.

In one direction down King Street, all the residential houses pop up and spread out as far as the eye can see. The houses off King Street, which are hidden behind all the shops on Main Street, stretch out for miles. Up the other direction on Main, he can see all the way to downtown. Small apartments and office buildings continue to grow until the largest, towering buildings of downtown, the

Grand Hotel, the executive and government buildings, take over the horizon.

Evyn stands on the corner of the intersection, wondering why it is so quiet in the middle of the day. There are no cars driving by and no people out and about. There is not a soul in sight. Evyn begins to worry. He wonders if the men in dark suits have returned to collect more people and steal their energy for themselves.

Finally, after looking in all directions several times and contemplating the possibility of another nightmarish encounter with the strange beings, Evyn spots several groups of people up and down the streets.

On Main Street, a small group of kids is exiting the arcade. In the other direction, a coffee shop owner is wiping off the patio tables. A few cars roll by, and Evyn breathes a sigh of relief and starts off walking.

"Hello," Evyn says to the coffee shop owner as he passes by, but there is no response. Evyn assumes the shop owner is too busy to hear him. He thinks nothing of it and carries on walking up the street.

Up ahead, Evyn recognizes a friendly woman coming out of the grocery store with her young children.

"Hi there. Nice day, isn't it?" Evyn says as he passes by.

Again Evyn is met with silence.

Very peculiar, Evyn thinks as he makes his way down Main Street. He starts walking toward the side road that leads to his beautiful girlfriend's neighborhood.

Chloe Taylor is always on Evyn's mind. Her perfect blonde hair and dazzling smile leave Evyn as mesmerized and helpless as the first day he met her. He always feels at his best with her, and he never misses the chance to spend as much time with her as possible. Her charming personality and devotion to Evyn are only a couple of the reasons why their relationship has blossomed so perfectly. Walking to her house has become a daily tradition, but today will prove to be very much different.

Evyn notices a small group of people outside the sporting goods store. He approaches the group, convinced there is no use in saying anything at all, but the urge to be friendly and polite is overwhelming.

Evyn walks by a few salespeople and a father and son who look like they just bought new bikes. He says with a smile, "Hello. Nice day isn't it?"

And just like before, there is no response or acknowledgement that they heard Evyn at all. Evyn walks past them. He is done being nice, and he is even feeling a little insulted.

Evyn looks over his shoulder and begins to feel concerned and more than a bit scared. A familiar feeling returns from the year before with the strange men in dark suits. Everyone Evyn has seen—everyone he had said hello to—is following him.

Their faces look repulsive, angry, and hostile. Their steps begin to quicken as soon as Evyn looks at them. Their menacing glares stab at Evyn like red-hot knives.

Evyn feels the most overwhelming flight-or-fight sensation. All his instincts are yelling at him to run! He starts to walk faster away from the crowd, and he calls out, "What's wrong? Can I help you? What's wrong with you?"

The angry people who are following him don't respond. The small crowd quickly grows into a large mob, and Evyn's walking quickly turns into running. He begins to run from the mob of furious people who are chasing him.

Evyn is very afraid of the unruly mob pursuing him. The growling pack grows in numbers and closes in on him. With no idea why they are chasing him—or why they refuse to answer his calls of reason—he shouts, "What do you want? Why are you chasing me?"

There is still no response. Looking back over his shoulder, Evyn catches a glimpse of their faces as he runs down Main Street.

The mob is furious, and they seem bloodthirsty. Their faces become contorted, and their mouths show large sinister grins of sharp teeth and scowling jaws. Their soft, healthy skin turns sickly shades of gray and green, and their eyes bulge and become bloodshot with rage. Evyn cannot make sense of anything.

Fear is all that's left in Evyn, and it settles in and takes hold of him. In a panic, he takes flight and runs with all the energy he can find. He can feel the adrenaline surging as he rounds the corner. The all-too-recognizable instinct has helped save his life so many times before.

Evyn rounds the corner of Main Street at full speed, and he stops in his tracks suddenly, almost falling forward. His heart is pounding so hard in his chest it feels like it might burst.

The road in front of Evyn is blocked and filled with another sea of crazed people, similar to those who have been chasing him. There must be hundreds—if not thousands—of them filling the streets. The people look hideous, repulsive, and evil. Their clothes are tattered and torn, and their faces are ghoulish and sinister. They stand around aimlessly, looking about in all directions.

Evyn stops on the street corner, and suddenly, every one of the disgusting, creepy people turn their heads to stare directly at him. Just like the crowd quickly closing in on him from behind, their bodies and faces begin to contort, turning lifeless, and sinister with rage.

In an instant, they quickly run at Evyn. Their hands reach out like claws, and Evyn can see their sharp teeth, and he can hear their snarling growls like wild animals. Like a dark storm cloud, thick with the blackness of death, the zombie creatures surround Evyn, closing in on him.

Through the cloud of darkness surrounding him, from within the mess of clawing hands reaching for him, the deafening moans and growls and through the putrid scent of decay, Evyn hears a familiar voice.

"Evyn, honey. Wake up! It's time to get ready for school." Evyn's mother's beautiful, melodic voice beckons him, and he snaps awake from the nightmare. Never has her voice been such a welcome sound.

"Thank God ... it was just a nightmare." Evyn finds himself in his room. His heart pounds in his chest as he gasps for breath, and the morning sun gleams in through his window.

Up until now, my life has been somewhat plain. It hasn't been completely uneventful, but I could always count on the predictability of it. Without question, the strange invasion, which took place earlier last year, allowed me to step up and prove I was stronger and braver than anyone thought possible. It was definitely a new and exciting experience to me. I was no longer afraid to take a stand and show determination when faced with the challenge of a seemingly impossible task. For the first time ever, I felt confident.

It is not often that people are given so many opportunities to persevere in the face of adversity, to stand up and challenge hardships, and to face and overcome their fears. Most people would simply accept what is out of their control and learn to live with it.

I have only just began to face the challenges in my life, and I am not even close to understanding what lies before me. For several weeks now, not much unlike my nightmare, I have been staring at a new and seemingly impossible task: my second year of high school.

High school was no breeze; it was much more difficult and required much more homework and studying than any previous years of school. Finding time to see Chloe or my friends has become more and more difficult as well. The time-consuming days and nights of keeping up on reading, research, and projects keeps me very busy and isolated at times.

Chloe Taylor is also very overwhelmed with the challenges of high school. She has undertaken her role on the student council, alongside her best friend Jennie, with such dedication that she has trouble finding time, if any at all, to herself. Chloe's cheerful best friend Jennie helps her with as much as she can. She takes notes during council meetings, she helps plan for all the school's social gatherings and with her outgoing, positive attitude, Jennie even heads up Chloe's campaign for student body president. She designs and wallpapers the halls of the school with posters of Chloe's smiling face and clever slogans, such as, "Vote for Chloe, your next Student President" and "Chloe's #1." Chloe and Jennie are glued together almost all the time. As social planners of Sir Arthur Wilfred High School, they rarely have a second apart from each other.

The one great thing—pretty much the only thing—that I really look forward to and enjoy more than anything about high school is when I get the chance to spend time alone with Chloe. I know I have the most amazing girlfriend I could ever hope for. Chloe and I have been inseparable all summer. We have become best friends and are happily fully-fledged boyfriend and girlfriend. And it doesn't hurt my popularity to have such a great girl by my side. But now that school is in full swing, we hardly get to spend more then a few hours together on weekends and the occasional rushed 'hello' between classes.

Besides my growing popularity from having such a great girlfriend, I have also taken all the practice we had running from the alien invaders and mastered my marathon skills. I was quickly becoming the school's next big track star. I am second to only one other student in astounding feats of speed. The much older boy is graduating soon and will leave me as the fastest student in all of Sir Arthur Wilfred High School.

My best friend Sam has taken up a position on the football team. Early in the morning before school starts, the football team practices nearby the track-and-field team. Such early morning practices have become all too exhausting to Sam and I, now playing on separate sports teams but a welcome gathering before a long hard day of school. I had hoped to join the football team with my best friend Sam but I just wasn't quite big or tough enough ... not yet.

I step out onto the track for my early morning run as I have every morning this year. I can see Sam across the field, breaking from the huddle and setting up for a practise play. My feet hit the ground one after the other, circling the field along the track. I see Sam grab the football off the hike; he takes a few steps back and scans the field for an opening. He throws the ball with such a force, it sails perfectly spiralling through the air and lands with pin point perscion into the hands of his fellow team mate.

Sam smiles with confidence and looks over at me. I smile with pride for my best friends achievements making second starting quarterback. Just then, distracted by Sam, my feet catch a rut in the track and I topple over myself. Sam squints, feeling my pain, the embarrassment is alright as I hope he was the only person who wintnessed my fall. I hop up quickly, brush myself off, and wave as I call out, "I'm okay." And I carry on with my run.

The bright yellow school buses line up outside Sir Arthur Wilfred High School as they do every morning. Only this year they will not be dropping me or my friend Sam, as we must now find other ways to get to school much earlier. I often walk or rely on the public transit system.

Newport's public transit system is nothing like the big city's system of dirty buses covered with odd smells, colorful graffiti, and numerous, extensive routes throughout the dense city. Newport has only a few routes and clean, well-maintained buses. Riding the bus to school every day was the least of my worries.

Not much else has changed over the summer. The sea of students has grown as a new generation of junior high students has been added to the masses of kids. My friends and I, now with our pick of the tables in the middle of the cafeteria, no longer have to sit near the crowded entrance or anywhere near those dreadful large garbage bins next to the lunch line.

Aside from all the extra hard work and time-consuming studying, high school has become much more enjoyable for me. Today is no exception. My favorite class—including Sam and Chloe—is going on a field trip to the museum of history.

The long-awaited history class trip, which I have been very

much looking forward to all month, was all set to depart the school just after lunch. I couldn't wait to see the wonderful exhibits and be immersed into a long forgotten world. *I really need a break from being stuck in the boring classrooms. This is going to be the best Friday ever!*

CHAPTER 2

FIELD TRIP

The students all linger outside the front of the school, waiting for the bus to take us to the museum. My best friends dad joins the classes as we wait.

"So, are you kids as excited as I am to learn about the history of ancient cultures?" Mr. Desjardins asks.

Sam's dad, Mr. Desjardins, had been all too eager to volunteer as a chaperone, as he was very interested in the new exhibit at the museum. With ancient cultures, old magic, witch doctors, kings of folklore, and the dark ages, the museum had recently opened the new exhibit featuring statues, relics, and all sorts of old books and paintings.

I am very excited, perhaps as excited as Mr. Desjardins. All the other students do not show as much interest, as they know how boring and stuffy museum field trips can be. But as the trip provides a break from the everyday, I look forward to it more than the mind-numbing schoolwork they would otherwise be doing in classrooms.

The school bus comes around the corner and parks in front of the waiting crowd of students. The door swings open and the kids begin piling in. We load into the bus, laughing and joking around as we take our seats. Mr. Desjardins speaks to the students from the front of the bus.

"Okay, everyone, settle down. Please take your seats and listen carefully. We're all grown-ups, I don't need to tell you how you're expected to act at the museum. You all have your work to do while you're there, so make sure you get it done and have fun. Enjoy the break from school, but don't forget you are representing the high school today."

The bus pulls out from the school and starts off through the city of Newport. It passes the shopping mall and crosses the downtown core. On the other side of the city, the large museum rests in the oldest section of the city.

As one of the oldest buildings in the city, the Museum of History was designed to outlast time. Renovated from an old affluent family house, the museum resembles a small castle. With its turn of the century design and immense size, it was built to last forever. With such attention to detail, and built by the wealthiest family of its time, no expense was spared. The best craftsmen must have taken years perfecting the large stone brick walls, the gothic cathedral moldings, and the old-style rooftops made of folded metal sheets and copper fixtures. It has required several renovations over the years to be modernized, but this historical landmark has been kept alive for centuries.

The bus pulls up to the historical museum, coming to a stop on the street out front. The kids all step out onto the old brick walkway, and the tour guide greets us. He is an older gentleman, with short white hair and dressed in a blue blazer with the museum's crest on it.

"Welcome, everyone," he loudly declares. "I am Francis, your tour guide for the day. We have lots to show you, including the newest exhibit, which I understand you've been studying at school. In just a moment we will head inside. I hope you all enjoy yourselves on this trip back in time."

As the tour guide continues talking about the museum, the

new exhibit, and recently discovered relics, I notice a small bubble begin to grow on the guide's neck. No larger than a wart, the small bubble grows larger and darker, expanding and multiplying up his cheek and along his face. The rash of dark warts begins to pulsate and pop, spewing blood and pus from the bumps.

Stunned by the sudden decay, vividly and grotesquely appearing on the side of the tour guide's face, I fall back in fright. I gasp and feel completely grossed out and frightened by the ghostly sight. "Oh my God. What is that? Are you okay?" I ask.

My classmates stop and stare at my sudden outburst.

I am now sitting up after falling on the brick walkway outside the museum. Unaware that no one else can see this terrifying sight, I wonder why everyone is staring at me instead of the revolting rash on the tour guide's face. I take a second look at the guide and notice the horrific rash has completely cleared.

"I was going to ask you the same thing, young man." The tour guide says as he helps me to my feet, his complexion restored to a healthy glow.

Several students chuckle at my unusual outburst.

"You okay, buddy? What was that about?" Sam asks.

"I'm fine. Thanks. I just thought I saw something," I respond.

Chloe walks over and says, "Evyn, what happened? Are you feeling all right?"

"Yeah. It's okay. I could've sworn I saw something awful on that tour guide's face, but I guess it was nothing. Let's just enjoy today."

Entering through the large wooden doors of the museum, we are immersed into a long-forgotten world. The hallway is lined with massive stone slabs, and several shiny suits of armor are on display. The hallway resembles a corridor in King Arthur's castle.

In the grand lobby of the museum, elegant tapestries hang from the walls. Royal furniture and large paintings surround the lavishly decorated room. The huge ceiling has detailed carvings and large wooden beams.

A huge staircase leads up to the main exhibit rooms of the

museum. The class follows the tour guide up the wide stairs and through a large double door.

The tour guide says, "These relics and books we've collected were made by ancient voodoo witch doctors, warlords, and kings. They tell the story of cultures and empires that practiced dark rituals, black magic, and even human sacrifice as a way of life. It wasn't until much later, closer to present day, that cultures such as these were persecuted and chased into hiding, fading into history." The tour guide stops and coughs before continuing. "Unlike the zombies you've seen in the movies or on television, these zombies are the undead servants of their creators. Many of the stories here speak of obedient, mindless servants who follow any order without question. Soldiers, servants, and even loved ones were given the gift of immortality. But, at the same time, they were cursed to live forever as soulless creatures."

The objects in the room mesmerize and capture all of our attention, and the exhibit is fascinating. Glass display cases line the room. Behind the glass cases, there are gold statues with strange markings, artifacts made of gold, metal, and rare stones—some bound together to form sacrificial knives and blades—and ancient scrolls and drawings. One case, which makes Chloe step back in fright, is full of shrunken heads.

"Careful, Chloe. Don't get too close. It's contagious, you know," Sam says.

A few other students laugh, and Chloe's best friend Jennie smiles at Sam.

Chloe says, "Jennie, do you have a crush on Sam?"

"I don't know. Maybe."

"Well, he is single—and he's a great guy," Chloe says.

"I suppose it doesn't hurt that he's Evyn's best friend. We could totally all hang out together," Jennie says.

"It would make for a lot of fun this summer," Chloe adds.

The classes of students move on through the museum, continuing their tour.

Beyond the glass cases, a large table is covered with old books and paintings. They show images of angels battling demons and men cowering before darkness and praising the light. One item in particular stands out to me, a small book bound in old leather.

I examine the captain's journal. Its entries record the history of the captain's life, dating as far back as the Dark Ages and the black plague in the 1500s.

Resembling a spell book more than a journal, the detailed stories describe rituals of both dark and light magic alike. There are several intricate drawings of beautiful angels, their healing powers over men, dark horrific demons, and their destructive magic burning and killing the masses.

I examine the book further, unable to make sense of its old Latin words. Deeper into the pages, the words change from Latin to French, and the last several pages are in English. I learn of the troubles faced when creating servants of undead zombies. The ritual of saving life and giving eternal life, if done incorrectly, leaves the person a mindless, heartless monster. Left to roam the earth forever, the ghoulish decaying shell wanders for an eternity, searching for its soul. I find it very interesting but rather farfetched and unbelievable.

The tour guide notices my interest in the book. "It describes the ancient ritual of turning someone into a zombie. It is believed it once belonged to one of the first voodoo witch doctors to ever come to America."

Suddenly, a crowd of men enters the room, and the tour guide's explanation of the journal is cut short. Security guards in blue blazers with the museum's crest accompany the men.

The curator of the museum tries to hold back a very sickly cough. "Excuse me, everyone! Unfortunately, the museum is closing early today. Sorry for the short visit, but we will be open again tomorrow if you should wish to come back and see the many exhibits." The curator coughs quietly throughout his speech.

"Is something wrong?" Mr. Desjardins asks.

"No, nothing to worry about. An issue has come up with our shipping department that we need to address." The curator's vague explanation—and the concerned looks among the museum staff—leaves Mr. Desjardins very curious as the students begin leaving the museum.

CHAPTER 3

STRANGE ILLNESS

The bus arrives back at school and drops all of us off. I leave the school a short time later with Sam, feeling somewhat disappointed in the short visit to the museum.

"Maybe there was a bomb threat?" I say as a joke while we're walking home.

"Yeah. Maybe they realized how boring the museum is—and they were doing us a favor," Sam says with a chuckle.

Sam and I part ways, and I head home down Main Street. I open the door to my house, drop my backpack on the floor, and go into the kitchen. My dad is there, which is unusual because he usually doesn't get home until after five o'clock.

"Hey, Dad. What are you doing home? Where's mom?" I ask concerned.

My dad quietly coughs before answering. "Your mom wasn't feeling good, and she went to the doctor. I'm not feeling so good either, so I came home early. How was the museum today?" My dad coughs some more.

"Oh, it was all right. The ancient culture exhibit was pretty cool, lots of interesting things to see," I reply.

"I'm glad you had fun. Make yourself something to eat. I'm going to see if I can catch your mom at the doctor's office. Maybe I'll take her out for a nice dinner." My dad always likes to do nice things when mom's not feeling well.

I don't mind one bit. Now I am free to eat whatever I want for dinner.

Later that evening, long after the sun has set, the house phone rings. I answer it, and it's my mom. I was expecting to hear that my parents were having a nice dinner and would be home soon, but instead she sounds awfully tired and sick, coughing uncontrollably. "Evyn, honey, I don't mean to worry you, but the doctors think I've got a bad case of bronchitis. They transferred me to the hospital for testing. Your father is here with me, and we should be home soon."

"Oh no, Mom. That's terrible! Is there anything I can do for you?"

"No, dear. Just stay home. We'll be home before you know it."

"Okay, Mom. Hope you feel better. See you soon."

I suddenly feel very worried and alone in the empty house. I begin a long night of waiting by the phone. I decide to watch television to help pass the time until my parents get home.

I get lost in my favorite television shows and a late-night movie. As the night drags on, my eyes begin to feel heavier. I watch television for what feels like forever. Just as I begin to fall asleep, the late edition of the news comes on the screen.

The broadcaster recounts the top stories of the day before mentioning the weather and the local news. It isn't until a segment regarding the outbreak of the flu that I shake my head free of the sleepiness and begin paying attention.

The hospital is seeing more cases of the flu virus than ever before. They have seen so many cases in fact, that a health advisory warning appears on the news along with a request that should anyone feel any flu-like symptoms, they are to report immediately to their doctor or the hospital.

Very strange. I become more concerned for my parents after seeing the story and I realize how late it is. It wasn't like my mom and dad to stay out so late, not when they aren't feeling well and especially not on a work night. I decide to call my dad's cell phone.

I dial the number and wait patiently as it rings, and rings, and rings, until the voice mail picks up. I end the call and instantly try my mom's cell phone. The voice mail also answers on my mom's phone, which is troubling because I know my mom is never without her phone.

"Mom, it's Evyn. Where are you guys? Call me back or get home already." Sounding like a concerned parent calling a child, I find the role reversal humorous.

I quickly dismiss any concerns. I know my parents can take care of themselves, but the lingering idea of something going wrong stays in the back of my mind as I doze off on the couch.

I wake up the next morning to the ringing phone and banging on the front door. Shocked and startled by the sudden noises, I snap awake with a jolt. I grab the phone as I walk toward the front door.

I approach the banging door. Reaching for the handle—and becoming more frustrated and angry at the loud banging—I hear my dad's voice on the phone.

"Evyn! Where have you been? I've been calling all morning!" My dad continues talking without waiting for an answer, and I stop in his tracks to listen. "We're still at the hospital. Something very bad is happening! Don't go outside—and don't let anyone in the house. If you have to leave, just go straight to Sam's house. Don't talk to anyone. Wait for us there."

The chilling warning sends a frozen chill up my spine, lifting all the hairs on my neck and arms.

"Dad, what is it? What's happening?" I have never heard my dad sound so alarmed.

"People are very sick, son, and they're acting out in crazy, violent ways! Just stay inside! Your mother and I are okay. We're going to try to get home as soon as possible." My dad hangs up the phone.

The banging on the door starts up again, and heeding my dads warning, I walk to the front window to see who it is.

Outside, leaning on the door, the mailman is banging away on the door with one arm. His other arm is supporting him against the wall. He is holding a handful of envelopes. In his blue uniform, hunched over in a contorted painful slump, he bangs on the door over and over again. He tilts his head over to the window as I look out at him.

I jump back in fright, instantly shocked by the man's menacing and wretched appearance. The mailman looks very pale and very sick. Sweat drips from his face, and he coughs uncontrollably.

I have no idea what to do. After my dad's warning, I become more and more fearful of the mailman's banging. *How long will the mailman keep banging on the door? What is this strange sickness my dad warned me about?*

Frightened and beginning to panic, I quickly put on my shoes and grab my cell phone from its charger. I take another look out at the crazed mailman.

"Just leave the mail in the box!" I shout out to the mailman.

With no response from the mailman, the banging continues to echo through the house. I head for the back door while dialling Chloe's number.

Chloe wakes up in her room. The morning sun is streaming in through her lace curtains. It lights up her plush, violet sheets and brightens her pink bedroom. Her desk and dresser are covered in piles of clothes, reminding her of her mom's request to tidy up her room.

Chloe's cell phone rings with my distinct ring tone, and she smiles as she stretches out in her comfortable bed and reaches for her phone. Whatever happy dreams she was waking up from—any pleasant thoughts of talking to her loving boyfriend first thing in the morning, spending the day with him, or enjoying some quality time alone—come to an abrupt end.

She presses the accept call button, and is met with my panicked, frantic voice. She had not heard such panic in my voice since the altercations with the mysterious men in dark suits almost a year ago.

"Chloe! Are you okay?" I abruptly ask.

"Yes, Evyn. I'm fine. I'm just waking up. What's wrong?" Chloe replies, growing more worried.

"Something strange is going on! Something is really wrong with everyone! Not like the men in dark suits. This is a lot worse."

My response reminds Chloe of the men in suits and the secret invasion that almost took over the city. "What is it, Evyn? What's happening?" Chloe, now fully awakened by my warning, becomes more serious and concerned.

"Everybody is really sick. Please just stay inside. Lock your doors. I'll be there very soon. And Chloe ..."

"What, Evyn?"

"Whatever you do, don't talk to anyone. If you notice anything strange, just run."

Chloe, more frightened by my vague warning, gets out of bed, quickly gets dressed, and runs through her house. She calls for her mom and dad, but there is no answer. She continues to call out for her parents and becomes even more worried because her parents are always getting ready for work when she wakes up.

She rushes from room to room, calling for her parents, but her cries are met by silence. Her house is unusually quiet. Chloe becomes more afraid than she has been in a long time.

She turns the television to the local news channel to get some answers. She waits through boring segments about traffic jams and disturbing police scenes. All of a sudden, there is a loud banging on the front door. Her attention shifts from the television, and she begins to panic.

She slowly walks to the door as she tries to regain her composure before confronting whoever or whatever may be out there. Chloe cautiously approaches the front window and spies outside. A sudden sense of safety washes over her, and her fear fades away.

She sees me knocking on the door, as I'm looking around to make sure no one is following me.

Chloe opens the door, and I hurry into the entranceway.

I instantly hug Chloe with such relief that she is alright. I am overjoyed she hasn't fallen victim to whatever is happening. For just a moment, both of us forget our concerns.

"What is going on, Evyn?" she asks.

"I'm not really sure. Are you okay though?"

"Yeah. I'm fine, just shaken up. I don't know what's going on. I don't know where my parents are, and they're not answering their phones."

"It'll be okay, Chloe. I'm sure they're fine. But a lot of people are getting sick, and it's getting out of control." I notice the television in the background. "Is there anything on the news about it?" I ask.

"No. Not really, just regular news," Chloe replies.

"We should go over to Sam's. Maybe his dad will have some answers. He's friends with a bunch of people at the hospital."

Chloe gathers a few things into her purse and puts her shoes on.

As we approach the front door, we hear a loud thump coming from upstairs. Chloe and I stop in our tracks. We pause and look at each other.

"I thought you said your parents weren't here?" I ask.

"I checked their room, and I called everywhere for them." Chloe is frightened by the noise.

"Wait here. I'll go check it out." I quietly make my way up the stairs.

I open the door and enter her parents empty, silent room. Just as I turn to leave, there is another loud thump.

"Hello?" I curiously ask. "Who's there?"

There is no response.

A moment later, I hear another loud thump coming from her

parent's bathroom. I cautiously approach the bathroom door, and I can tell that someone—or something—is trying to get out. My hand trembles slightly as I reach for the doorknob. I feel prepared for whatever I may encounter behind the door, but I am also ready to slam the door shut and run for my life in an instant. Slowly, I turn the doorknob and swing the door open.

The door flies open, and I gasp in shock. Chloe's mom is not her usual, charming self. She is usually happy and beautiful; her blonde hair is always brushed, and her makeup is done just right. Instead, she is standing there with gray skin, baggy eyes, dirty clothes, and knotted, messy hair.

Chloe's mom stares at me for a moment with a confused expression. I do not believe what I see. In an instant, her gaze turns to torment and rage. She breaks out of her trance and lunges at me. Her eyes turn red as she reaches for me. I slam the door shut, trapping her inside the bathroom.

I remember what my dad told me, and I feel awful that Chloe's mom has fallen victim to this awful sickness. I rush downstairs, take Chloe by the hand, and pull her along as we head straight for the front door.

"What was that noise?" she asks.

"It's just the wind knocking a window," I answer. "Come on. We have to get over to Sam's house."

The two of us leave Chloe's house and begin the walk to Sam's house, just a few streets away. Our once leisurely stroll up the street to Sam's house is cut short as Chloe and I are taken aback by the sound of approaching thunder. It sounds like distant firecrackers, and the noise is getting louder.

"What is that? Can you hear it?" Chloe asks.

Resonating louder and louder as it comes pouring over the hills in the distance, I realize exactly what the noise is as I say, "It's helicopters."

A swarm of helicopters roar overhead. There are so many dark-green army helicopters flying fast and low. The whipping propellers drown out all other sounds in the area. Chloe and I stand there on the street as the helicopter motors scream like freight trains thundering by. The noise is deafening, Chloe and I can only watch with our hands over our ears as they quickly pass overhead.

"This can't be good. Come on, we should hurry!" I say.

Chloe and I waste no time and begin running toward Sam's house.

Sam and his dad are staring intently at the computer. Sam's dad had found some very strange bulletins on the Internet about the illness that is spreading across Newport, neighboring cities, and all over the state. Government officials have called for a complete quarantine at hospitals, and the unexplainable disease has prompted a national health advisory warning.

"This is crazy," Sam exclaims.

"I've never seen anything like it," Sam's dad says.

"Do you think it could be an attack?" Sam asks.

"What? Like terrorists? No. I don't think they could manage anything like this," Mr. Desjardins says. "Stay inside. Wait here for me. I'm going to talk to my friends at the hospital. Maybe I can help out and get some answers at the same time."

A few moments after Sam's dad drives away, the swarm of army helicopters roar by outside. They fly right over Sam's house and he runs to the window to catch a glimpse of them. Just then he sees me and Chloe rushing up to his house. Sam opens the door, signaling for us to hurry inside. He closes the door and quickly locks it behind us.

"Are you guys okay?" Sam asks as we rush inside.

"Yeah, we're fine. What about you?" Chloe responds.

"I'm good. I've been watching the news and trying to figure out what's going on. Were those army helicopters that just flew by?"

"Yeah. They were in a hurry. This disease must be something serious," I say.

"Good to see you're okay. Are you feeling all right? Have you run into any sick people today?" Sam asks.

"Yeah. We're fine," Chloe answers.

I can't bring myself to answer honestly, so I just drop my eyes to the floor.

"What is it, Evyn?" Sam asks.

"The mailman at my house today was really sick. I didn't open the door at all. My dad warned me not to. My mom and dad are at the hospital, and they told me that sick people have been acting crazy—violent even."

"I'm sure they're fine if they're at the hospital," Sam responds. "The best thing we can do is sit tight and wait to hear more about what's going on."

We do just that, and gather in front of the television and wait for any updates or new information.

Outside the hospital, a reporter talks about the overwhelming number of cases in Newport and the unusual symptoms of the disease. There is no new information about what the disease is, if there's a cure, where it came from, or how it spreads.

In the background, the hospital is bustling with soldiers in uniform and special disease control men in biohazard and quarantine suits.

Sam, Chloe and I are more worried than ever. Chloe keeps trying to contact her parents on their cell phones.

Sam and I know that things do not look good for anyone. I pull Sam aside and say, "I was over at Chloe's house earlier, but I didn't tell her about this. Her mom was trapped in the bathroom. She was really sick, and she attacked me when I tried to help her."

"I wouldn't tell Chloe about her mom, Evyn. I think it would only upset her more. My dad should be home soon. He went to look for answers at the hospital."

On the television, there are more warnings of the illness

spreading. The director of the hospital says, "The hospital has become overwhelmed with patients, and we have to start considering closing our doors to the sick."

In the background, army personnel and emergency staff begin running all over. Without warning, the news feed from the hospital stops. The television screen is filled with static. For a moment, we all stare in shock at the fuzzy screen.

The television switches back on. The anchorman in the news studio is shocked at the abrupt static from the hospital. "Sorry about that, folks. It seems we've lost our connection to our reporter in the field. Hopefully the hospital will figure out what's going on, and we'll get back to you soon with more information about this strange epidemic."

We continue to stare at the television. We are completely mesmerized and shocked by the chaotic scene. Our attention is distracted when the power goes out in Sam's house. Everything in the house shuts down. The television flicks off, and the lights go out.

"Oh no. This can't be good," Chloe says.

"Is it just your house—or is all the power out?" I ask.

"I have no idea," Sam replies.

We all walk over to the front of the house and look outside. We can't see much from looking out into the daylight. The streetlights haven't come on yet, and there's no sign of life. Just then, we see some of Sam's neighbors outside, also looking for answers.

We go outside, cautiously looking around to make sure there are no sick people anywhere.

Sam calls out to his neighbor. "Hey, is your power out?"

"Yeah. I'm guessing the power is out everywhere. There is no way to tell how bad it is unless we head into town. It's best to just stay inside and wait it out. I'm not going anywhere with this disease spreading everywhere," the neighbor answers.

We agree with the neighbors warning and go back inside the house.

It isn't long before Sam's dad arrives home. He coughs and sweats as he limps from the car and struggles his way to the front door. The door swings open, and Mr. Desjardins falls abruptly to the floor.

Sam rushes over to his dad. "What's wrong? What happened?" Sam helps his dad to his feet.

"It's not good, Sam. Something is very wrong," Mr. Desjardins says as he coughs. He is too weak to walk and collapses again.

"Dad, what happened? How did you get sick?" Sam asks, very concerned.

"It's not a disease, Sam. Something else is causing this. It's like a nightmare out there," Sam's dad says. "Doctors aren't able to explain it. Even the government specialists are baffled by whatever it is. You kids need to get out of here. Go somewhere safe and hide. Stay hidden. Take food and supplies—and just wait it out. Wait until you hear something."

"Are you serious, Dad? Where are we supposed to go? What can we do?" Sam asks.

"Just go, Sam! Get to Evyn's house. And stay safe." Mr. Desjardins starts coughing wildly. He coughs, grips his chest in agony, and collapses onto the floor.

Chloe and I are so shocked we can not help but stare in silence, as Sam rushes over to help his dad.

"Dad! Dad, are you okay? Come on. Get up!" Sam leans down to help his dad.

Mr. Desjardins abruptly stands up and grabs Sam's arm.

I already know what's coming, but it's too late to do anything.

Mr. Desjardins grip is cold. His bloodshot eyes bulge from his head. His face turns slightly green, and a strange black rash begins to grow up the side of his neck and face.

"Dad?" Sam curiously asks.

His dad's gaze turns horrifying, cold, and ghostly. His face has no expression, and his mouth forms an evil grin. His mouth opens wide and he begins to cough wildly, violently spraying a foul-smelling black liquid all over Sam.

I begin to move Chloe toward the front door, as she just looks on in horror.

Sam screams and tries to wipe the liquid from his face.

Mr. Desjardins continues contorting and coughing toward Sam.

Sam begins to cough uncontrollably. His eyes begin to burn, and a dark black rash starts to form on his hands and face.

Chloe and I stare helplessly at our best friend. We both feel awful that there is nothing we can do for our friend, and we quickly leave the house.

I know it's too late to help, as I pull Chloe out the front door, and we start running.

CHAPTER 4

LIVING NIGHTMARE

As quietly as possible, Chloe and I hide in my parent's attic. The trusted shelter of the attic has served as a safe haven for me before. The two of us are quiet, shocked, and horrified by the nightmare that is taking over Newport.

Birds are chirping outside, and the wind is blowing in the trees. Far up the road, almost near Main Street, we can hear garbage cans being knocked over and retching moans. The noise echoes loudly and painfully through the nearly deserted streets.

When the noise stops, the streets become silent again. The silence is more frightening than either of us thought possible, and we listen even more closely.

The tormented moans start again. The grunting and garbled wails of the sick people slowly move up the street. The moans get louder as the sluggish people get closer.

I stand up to look out the small attic window.

"No, Evyn," Chloe whispers.

"It's okay. I just want to see what's out there."

I almost wish I hadn't. A horde of mindless zombies fills the street, dragging their feet and staggering. Their ragged clothes are covered with the wretched black liquid. Their skin is green and grey, and they're covered in repulsive black rashes.

"We have to get out of here," I say, trying to hide my concern as best as I can.

"Where are we supposed to go? The last warning on TV said to stay inside and avoid this thing. Help will come soon, Evyn. Please. Let's just stay inside and wait."

"I know you're scared, Chloe. I am too. But we can't just wait around, hoping to be saved. It's just like what happened with the aliens. Remember how scared we were? There was nobody coming then—and we don't know if there will be anyone coming now."

"We don't know anything for sure, Evyn. Those army helicopters may have been carrying soldiers and people who can help us. We don't know what's going on or how far it has spread. They might already have a cure. If we stay here, we stand a better chance."

"Chloe, we have to find out what's going on. We'll stay safe and hidden, but we can't stay here."

We gather bottles of water, some food, a small radio, a blanket, and our cell phones, and we quietly go downstairs.

The horrible moaning continues outside. Outside, huge crowds of repulsive zombies march along aimlessly.

"Look at them. Where are we going to go, Evyn?" Chloe asks.

"Maybe we should go to the hospital? If there is any chance of a cure and finding help, it would be there."

"How are we ever going to make it there through this? And you saw the hospital on the news. It was chaos!"

"It was the last place my parents called me from," I say.

Chloe and I wait for the zombies to vanish up the street before we exit the house and start making our way toward downtown.

Chloe and I do not see a soul in sight, not until we start walking down Main Street. People look helplessly out of their windows, hiding in fear. The remaining healthy people are smart enough to stay hiding inside and out of sight. *How many people have already turned into these mindless creatures?* I think to myself.

Farther up the street, we spot a small group of people. I hesitate for a moment before calling out to them. "Hey!" I shout out.

There is no response.

"Are you guys okay?" Chloe calls out.

There is still no response. The people suddenly tilt their heads toward the sound of our voices. With an evil scowl and squinty red eyes, they glare at me and Chloe.

"Oh no," I whisper. An overwhelming sense of fear takes hold of me. I grab Chloe by the hand and turn to run.

All of a sudden, crowds of zombies with green skin, red eyes, and menacing grins start moving toward Chloe and me. They stagger out of alleyways, and doorways, and out from around corners, their mouthes and teeth dripping with the same disgusting black venom, and that smell. I have never smelled anything so rank in my whole life. The putrid scent of decay and death was everywhere. It fills both Chloe's and my nostrils with a stink like nothing we have ever smelled before. We both cringe at the disgusting odor, and we try to block our noses as we run.

Monstrous cries emanate from down the street. Wretched growls and moans come out from alleyways and buildings. Chloe and I keep running as our lives depend on it. The zombies are everywhere.

With no easy escape in sight, we keep running away from the gathering monsters. We run across the street and off into the city along Main Street. The small group of zombies behind us grows larger as more join the herd. We run toward Fashion Island shopping mall. It is a haven from the nightmare of the open streets.

As we round the last corner off Main Street, mine and Chloe's spirits lift at the sight of the mall and we begin to run even faster. I really hope that the shopping mall, which we know inside and out, will offer us protection and salvation even if just for a little while.

It doesn't take very long for the lifeless, contorted zombies to arrive at the mall. Chloe and I burst through the large shopping mall doors. Behind us, the mob of ghoulish creatures has attracted many more of the stench-ridden monsters. A huge crowd of beasts now heads straight for us and the mall.

Chloe and I run all the way along the first floor. It looks very much different than the mall we remember. The power is off. There is nothing but old food and dusty debris being lit up by the light shining through the large skylight windows.

The shopping mall has fallen victim to the disease. Evacuated and left to rot, with no one left to properly clean it or take care of anything, everything is filthy. That same stench of decay rests very heavy in the air. The smell is very disheartening, but we have to hurry, there's no time to worry about the stench.

The mall had no hope. When the healthy people evacuated, they left everything in an unorganized mess. The sick and infected were left behind, trapped, and they trashed everything.

The shopping mall is now a tomb. Looters never even bothered coming here. They know the infection is spreading much too rapidly.

A few scattered zombies notice Chloe and me quickly moving along. The monsters begin to stagger toward us.

"Come on. We have to keep moving and find somewhere safe to hide!" I say. "The mall may not be the best hiding place."

We move quickly through the abandoned shopping mall. Everything looks much worse than the empty mall they witnessed when aliens in dark suits invaded. This is no alien invasion—this is a zombie outbreak.

Chloe and I make our way up through the floors, hoping to find shelter in the dark nightmare that is now the shopping mall. With the zombies steadily entering through the front doors and their numbers quickly multiplying, we make haste and enter a store up on the third floor. We quickly lock and barricade the door behind us.

"We should be safe here for a while. I don't think they know how to open doors." I quickly check that the back door is locked.

"What are we going to do, Evyn?" Chloe asks.

"I'm not sure, but we need to rest for a bit. I'll try to think of something." My optimistic answer doesn't comfort Chloe as much as she hoped it would.

"Remember the last time we had to hide in the bed and bath store? We had all sorts of comfy blankets and pillows," Chloe says.

"Yeah. I was almost more scared then, but this is feeling pretty close," I say.

Chloe looks around the store. "As long as we're in a clothes store, we should pick out some things we like. You could use a change of clothes too."

"Very funny, but you're right. I have been sweating in these all day."

We both find some clothes we like and step into the changing rooms to try them on. We come out and feel much better in clean, dry, comfortable clothes.

That night, Chloe and I try to relax in the back corner of the clothing store.

All of a sudden, my cell phone rings loudly, and the sound resonates through the entire store. Our faces turn pale, and our hearts sink into our bellies.

"Turn it off. Quick, answer it!" Chloe says.

I dig my phone out of my backpack, it's my dad calling. "Dad? Where are you? Are you and Mom okay?" There is no answer. I can only hear muffled sounds and a strange rustling. My dad has accidentally pocket-dialed me.

"Dad!" I call out again, hoping for some sign of life—or any response at all—but it was too late.

A loud thump comes from the front door of the srore, followed by scratching, banging, and sinister moans. My phone had attracted a group of zombies, and they are trying to get into the store.

"Wait here a second, Chloe." I say as I make my way to have a look.

The zombies begin to gather outside the store. All it took was one to get excited and the rest were attracted to it. Most of them claw and climb over one another to get in, while others linger about outside the store.

The weak glass of the front display window comes crashing down beneath the weight of the creatures. The zombies trip over one another as they climb into the store.

I run as fast as I can to the back of the store. "Quick! Grab your stuff. We've got to get out of here!"

I grab my backpack and race for the back door. The employee door which leads to the concrete maze of access hallways.

Chloe and I burst through the door and race down the hallway. The cement echoes with our footsteps as we run.

We round a corner and look for a safe exit. As we push open a large door, a crowd of zombies block our path ahead.

All the sick and infected employees of the mall must have been trapped in the access hallways. With no escape in sight, both of us turn and keep running. The brick walls and concrete floors seem to go on forever.

Chloe and I round a corner and to no surprise we see more zombies ahead of us. We look behind, and our path is blocked on both ends.

Like a shining ray of light, we see an escape. A solid metal door marked: *Roof Access, Emergency Only, Locks Behind You*. With a sturdy push on the metal handle, we shove the door open and hurry outside. The door locks tightly behind us.

Chloe and I are now trapped on the empty rooftop. With the door locked securely behind us, we look out over the edge of the roof. The sea of monsters in the parking lot—and surrounding the entire shopping mall—horrifies us. We move back, shocked, stumbling slowly away from the ledge.

Chloe stands very still. She tries not to add to the frightening situation. She doesn't make a sound and hopes for a sign of hope from me.

I try to gather my thoughts. I make my way to an oversized skylight. I stare down into the shopping mall. Zombies fill the shopping mall like water in an aquarium. They fill all three floors of the mall.

"Um, Chloe?" I signal for her to take a look.

The city seems so far away. There is almost a thousand yards between us and the safety of Newport's streets.

A leisurely stroll through the shopping mall was normal before the long walk home. We used to look forward to the walk home after a day at the mall, but thousands of hideous, unrelenting zombies blocked the way. *Has every person in the city changed? Are they all infected by this awful sickness? Are we all that remain?*

The zombies have no sense of what they're doing. They wander about with no control and no idea what's going on.

The zombies remind me of the bustling crowds of shoppers—and they aren't that different. I think of healthy people frantically moving about—stressed, confused, and overwhelmed by the large shopping mall—as they try and get their shopping done.

Chloe and I stare down at the massive amount of ungodly monsters swarming all over the mall. All hope seems lost, and I feel hopelessly defeated. Chloe slides her soft hand into mine and squeezes it gently. I look over into her beautiful, gleaming eyes, and she smiles.

I suddenly get an idea. The feeling of hope springs up again, and my spirit is lifted by Chloe's affections. My idea is not very grand or amazing, not even very good, but it might just be a chance for us to escape this nightmare. I walk over to the corner of the roof. "I just got a weird idea. Bear with me." I reach down and scoop up a pile of muck, old rainwater, and dirt that has collected along the corners of the roof.

"If we smear this stuff all over ourselves, maybe we can blend in with the zombies. Maybe we can walk right by them without them even noticing us."

"That's disgusting. I think you've watched too many zombie movies. It might not work, but I guess it doesn't hurt to try."

Chloe reluctantly agrees with the dirty plan. We cover ourselves with dirt and muck, smearing it all over our clothes, arms, and legs.

"Evyn, don't move," Chloe says.

I look up from wiping the wet mud and dirt on my legs and get a face full of the sticky slime from Chloe. She wipes it all over my face. I can't help but smile and squirm at the gross muck, trying to keep it away from my mouth.

"Don't be such a baby. It was your idea," Chloe says as her smile turns into a laugh.

Chloe and I feel much more confident once we have a plan and some hope for escape. We very much resemble the dirty zombies we have been running from. The stench is awful, the muck is everywhere, and we both now feel brave and strong once again. Chloe and I come alive with the hope of escaping the masses of moaning monsters below.

"Are you ready?" I ask.

She pulls me close and kisses me for good luck. "As ready as I'll ever be."

"We have to move slowly. Try to pretend we're just a couple of zombies. Follow me and stay close." We walk over to an emergency stairwell. I reach out and open the door.

The stairs are empty. No zombies have found their way into the stairwell. Chloe and I quickly and quietly climb down the three flights of stairs. We pause before opening the doors at the bottom and listen carefully to the quiet moans and shuffling on the other side.

We open the door slowly and are confronted by the swarms of zombies; the mall is full of them. *The smell is disgusting.*

"Follow me," I whisper as I block my nose.

I take Chloe by the hand and we slowly creep along the wall

toward the closest exit. We avoid the slow zombies and pause whenever one crosses our path.

My plan seems to be working. The creatures take no notice of us two mud-covered kids as we stagger our way through the mall.

I lead the way, looking for any open path and slowly weaving between the crowds of zombies, trying desperately to keep a safe distance from them.

The moaning and grunting of the lifeless creatures blends into a single horrible noise and it starts to hurt Chloe's ears. She begins to think of all these people as they once were and she wonders if they will ever once again be normal humans. Chloe bursts into tears when she realizes how dreadful it is. How all these people may never recover or be how they once were.

"Don't look at them, Chloe," I whisper. "We're almost there."

After a few close calls, we make it to a side exit to the underground parking lot and escape unharmed. The parking lot looks empty. It seems safe for now, but we know there are zombies surrounding the mall. We walk quickly through the parking garage.

Suddenly, the zombies come from all directions. As the zombies begin to flood from the mall behind us, Chloe and I start running once again. We run with all our might toward the city.

Chloe and I are exhausted, but adrenaline keeps us moving at an astounding pace. We run down the city streets and through alleyways. We did not expect there to be so many of them. Thousands of zombies slowly chase us into the city.

I try to concentrate as the sweat on my muddy head starts to drip into my eyes and the painful burning in my legs begins to weaken me. *How will we ever find a safe place? How will we ever find answers or other survivors?*

In the shadows of a dimly lit alleyway, we try to formulate a plan after losing the zombies. When we walk out onto Main Street, we freeze. There are zombies everywhere! All over the filthy streets, groups of menacing zombies wander about aimlessly. Some stand still, some stagger about, and others wander along the street without direction. We have no idea what to do, and our muddy disguises have began to fade.

"Maybe they don't realize we're not like them," Chloe says.

The zombies start walking toward us. Completely exhausted, Chloe and I run toward an old industrial building. We are confident we can escape the slow group of zombies following us, but just as we climb the large concrete steps outside the front of the building, fatigue catches up with me.

I stagger and trip on the stairs, and my head smashes against the top step. A deafening ringing in my ears drowns out the moaning zombies in the distance and Chloe frantically calling out my name. Everything goes silent and seems to grow darker. The last thing I see as I fall unconscious is a pair of very small legs running to help Chloe and another pair of small legs running toward the zombies. I slip into blackness.

CHAPTER 5

THE HIDEOUT

When I wake up, a boy with messy brown hair and tattered clothes is staring at me. A young girl with long, messy brown hair hides behind the boy.

"You think he's one of them?" the little girl asks.

"Nah. He doesn't really look like a zombie," the boy responds.

"Maybe he's sick like the others?" the girl says.

"We'll know soon enough," the young boy responds.

The boy and girl jump up and run out of the room as I begin to wake up. A few moments later, a teenage boy walks into the room. "Welcome back, Sleeping Beauty."

I try to sit up.

"Take it easy. You've got a really nasty cut on your head."

"Where am I? How long have I been asleep? Where's the girl I was with?" I slowly remember what happened.

"Don't worry about anything. Chloe is in the other room, and she's perfectly fine. You've been out for a whole day. You must have really needed the sleep."

The boy's statement makes me rest a little easier. "Who are you? Where am I?" I realize I am a guest in someone's hideout.

"My name is Richard. For now, this is what I like to call home. I found this place while looking for somewhere to hide when the sickness first started spreading. I was running from a group of sick people, and I stumbled into this old building. I realized how protected it was. I was able to hide here for quite some time. It's got its own generator, and there is so much space. When I went out to look for supplies, I found some friends, and they stay here too."

I stand up and properly greet Richard. He is tall and strong with dark brown hair and an innocent smile. He reminds me a lot of Sam.

"My name is Evyn. Thank you for saving us."

"I know who you are, Evyn. Chloe told us all about you. And don't thank me. It was the twins who saved you guys. They heard the zombies and Chloe's voice outside, and they came to your rescue before the rest of us could make it."

"Who's 'the rest of us'?" I ask as we walk out into an old studio apartment.

"We've managed to save a lot of lost kids. Some of the older kids are out looking for supplies and people who might need saving, but the youngest kids are all here staying safe."

There are kids everywhere in the apartment. A lot of them are up on the second floor or hanging out in the balcony. Most of the children are down on the first floor hanging out, talking, reading, or playing games.

Richard and I exit one of the rooms on the second floor. The rooms have all been turned into bedrooms to accommodate everyone.

Sleeping areas are everywhere. Beds, cots, and sleeping bags are spread out across the entire apartment. A large supply of food and water is piled up against a wall near the kitchen area. A television, a large couch, and some chairs are set up in the middle of the apartment.

"Good morning, Evyn," Chloe happily calls out from the kitchen. Several young girls are helping her bake cupcakes for a big dinner she's preparing.

"Someone had to make sure these kids get a hot meal. If they had it their way, they'd live on junk food," Richard says.

Chloe and the girls start passing out plates. For the first time in days, the kids are happy.

"A hot meal is very important, isn't that right, Evyn?" Chloe's smile always melts my heart.

"Yes. Of course. Growing bodies need lots of good food," I awkwardly say.

The two young twins run up to me and Richard. They try to hold back their foolish excitement behind silly smiles.

"Hi, Evyn!" the girl says while blushing.

"We're the ones who saved you!" the boy adds.

"This is Mike and Marcy. They were the first to see you and Chloe in trouble. They rushed out, led the zombies away, and helped bring you inside. They probably should have waited for some older kids to help, but it's a good thing they didn't." Richard gives a stern look to the twins.

"My sister Marcy has a huge crush on you!" young Mike says.

"No, I don't! Why would you say that, Mike?"

Richard leads me down to the main floor. "When we first realized that everyone was turning into zombies, we hid here for a day. We had no idea what to do, but we started venturing out for supplies. We kept finding more kids out there. Most of their parents were sick, and the kids had nowhere else to go. Some were hiding in stores, others were left alone in cars, and a lot were afraid to go inside their houses because their parents had gotten sick and changed. We saved most of them while they were running from the zombies." Richard suddenly stops.

"What is it? What's wrong?" I ask.

"It's just that, with all the parents gone, I've kind of taken on the role of a parent around here. I'm not sure what to do." Richard takes me over to an alcove with a large bay window overlooking the city. The window lets in a lot of bright sun, which lights up the apartment. The window offers a vast view of the city which now looks desolate. No busy streets, no sounds or cars, no birds or noises of any kind. There's so much smoke, it billows in the distance and rises up everywhere like pillars to the sky. The city of Newport looks like the aftermath of war.

Off to one side of the apartment, the bay window alcove offers some privacy from all the young kids. Richard continues explaining to me. "I followed the helicopters to the hospital. I was hoping to find some help or some answers, but what I found was awful. The hospital was a war zone. It was complete mayhem. Sick people were everywhere. Even the soldiers were getting sick, and then everything went crazy. Everyone was becoming infected and turning into zombies. Everyone tried to run, but the infection was spreading too fast. Some tried leaving in the helicopters. They were infecting one another, and there was no escape for anyone. All I could do was watch in horror from a nearby rooftop. The helicopters came crashing down and burst into flames. Then I saw *him* … this strange man. This rich guy in a nice suit comes walking out of the hospital without a care in the world. He seemed healthy, calm, and happy. Then I saw something I wasn't expecting at all—and that's what made me follow him. I still don't believe it and can't understand it, but as he walked away from all the chaos and carnage at the hospital, the zombies started to follow him. Like servants, they just followed him all the way up the street. I even saw him send groups of them off in different directions. I followed the man until he looked right at me. There was no way he could know I was up there on the rooftop, but he looked right at me. I jumped down the fire escape and hid on another roof. After that, I lost him in the city. I guarantee he knows something really important about all this. The zombies never touched him. They listened to him and followed his commands. It was the creepiest thing I've ever seen."

Chloe walks up and says, "Evyn's seen some really creepy things."

"Where was the last place you saw him?" I ask.

"Quite a few blocks up from the hospital, just near the Grand

Hotel. Why? You're not thinking of going looking for him, are you?" Richard asks.

"We have to do something. We have to find answers," I exclaim.

Suddenly, everyone's attention is drawn to three teenage boys coming into the apartment through an upstairs window. They climb in from the fire escape and make their way down to the first floor. They unload their backpacks and bags of supplies and walk over to Richard, Chloe and me.

"Are you guys okay? You've been gone since yesterday," Richard asks the boys.

"Yeah. We're fine. We got tied up in the city. We had to spend the night on top of the big grocery store. We didn't touch a single sick person," one of the boys says.

"We have some new guests. Who are they?" another boy asks.

"We saved them shortly after you guys left yesterday. This is Evyn Hunter and Chloe Taylor. Evyn and Chloe, this is Paul, Matt, and Erik. Paul and I were the first to find this building and secure it as a hideout. Matt and Erik are the best at traveling unseen through the city. They were the first to take to the rooftops and fire escapes."

Paul says, "While we were collecting supplies from the grocery store, we heard the swarm coming. There must have been about a hundred zombies, but we noticed something really strange this time, something we have never seen before. There were two types of zombies out there."

Matt says, "We get up to the roof and spy out over the edge. There's a huge swarm of creepy, dirty zombies staggering up toward the store. All of a sudden, another group of zombies walks up and starts pushing and shoving their way through."

Erik adds, "Don't forget about how it took forever."

Matt says, "I'm getting to that part. We must have been up on that roof for hours. The sun starts going down, and these zombies are actually fighting with one another! It's hard to explain."

Paul continues, "We haven't seen zombies like these before.

They were actually sort of clean. They didn't have the same dirty clothes or green skin. They were actually trying to gather the creepy zombies together like sheep. They were trying to herd them toward the city. The creepy zombies wouldn't do it; they wouldn't budge. The clean zombies kept trying though. They were grunting, shoving, and trying to move the scary zombies. All the zombies became angrier, and they were walking wherever they wanted. They were moaning and snarling like they always do. It was kind of ridiculous to watch."

Everyone listening in the apartment tries to make sense of what they are hearing.

"What else did you guys see?" I ask.

"We just waited and waited. After the moaning stopped, we saw them all walking off toward downtown. When the coast was clear, we made our way back here," Paul says.

I take Chloe aside. "I'm going to check something out in the city."

"Are you crazy, Evyn? You can't go out there by yourself!"

"I need you to stay here. You have to stay safe. You know I'm fast. I'll stay hidden. I have an idea, and I need to find out what's going on."

"What's your brilliant plan?" Chloe asks.

"I'm going to make my way toward the city to try to find the man who was controlling the zombies."

"Seriously? That sounds stupid," Chloe says.

Richard interrupts and says, "No. Actually, it sounds pretty smart. To be honest, if we are able to find the largest concentration of zombies, they should lead the way to that man they saw—and maybe to some answers."

"It sounds like you guys have a death wish to me!" Chloe exclaims.

"We can help," Paul adds.

Paul, Matt, and Erik are happy to volunteer. The three of them have always been tough kids, and they find it fun to venture into the city, hiding, and traversing rooftops and fire escapes, and staying one step ahead of the zombies.

"What are you going to do if you find the zombies? It's not like they will lead you right to that man," Chloe says.

Matt says, "We will explore the city and look for the largest amount of zombies we can find. We'll lure the creatures away and somehow find the strange man. We can get some answers from the mysterious man who controls the zombies."

"Come on lets eat. We can talk more about it soon." Chloe puts a stop to the conversation. I think she is very concerned about the plan.

When the younger kids have gone to sleep after dinner, all of the older kids gather in the living room.

"We'll leave first thing in the morning." Richard gives me an emergency backpack with food, water, a first-aid kit, and other important survival gear. "Most important, do not let the zombies touch you. A scratch or a bite will make you change fast—and even a cough will spread the nasty black venom."

"I've seen it firsthand. My best friend got attacked by his own dad—right in front of us," I say.

"If you get trapped, use this." Richard passes me a very powerful flashlight. "Shine it right in their eyes. It blinds them like crazy. They're very sensitive to bright light, and it might just save your life."

Chloe pulls me aside in the kitchen and says, "Evyn, I'm really worried about you. If you go out into the city, who knows what will happen, you might end up like those things, like a zombie."

"I'll be fine Chloe, I'll be more careful than I've ever been." My reassurance does not help convince Chloe.

"You can't know for sure Evyn. What about your parents, or our friends? You saw what happened to Sam. I can't imagine losing you too Evyn?"

"I promise I'll be extra careful. There's no way I'm losing you but I've got to do something, I've got to help. I promise I'll be back before you know it."

I try to calm Chloe's worries and reassure her I don't want anything to happen to me as much as she does. I have to go find answers. I have to do something.

This plan sounds crazy. I don't want you going, but I understand that you have to help." Chloe tries not to cry as she says good night. She gives me a big hug and a kiss and goes off to a bedroom with the other girls.

I try to sleep. *What a strange world this has become. It is great to see these kids are safe, helping one another and looking out for one another under such horrible circumstances.* I can't help but feel lucky to not be alone while facing this terrifying zombie threat. I start to miss Sam and worry about my parents. I roll over onto the couch and smile for the first time in a while—knowing there may be hope—before I fall asleep.

In the morning, the boys and I leave the safety of the hideout. The rooftops offer a lot of help in getting us into the city. The boys have set up makeshift bridges and use ropes to swing across the gaps between buildings. When they reach a building that is too far to swing across, they head for the fire escape. Climbing down the rusty metal steps and ladder rungs to the ground below, we take a few steps across the alleyway and start climbing up the next fire escape.

"Evyn, these fire escapes come in very handy. We can make it almost all the way downtown along the rooftops," Paul says.

"This must help a lot when you have to make it to stores for supplies and stuff safely," I reply.

"Yeah, you can get pretty much anywhere in the city if you stay hidden. Just don't forget to always be on the lookout. The zombies could be anywhere," Matt adds.

The boys and I make our way downtown without seeing a single zombie. Everything is quiet. There is no moaning or grunting, and no zombies shuffling through the city. From every building, we carefully look out over the edges, expecting to see zombies. There is no one and nothing moving out on any of the streets.

Enormous office buildings and high apartments loom ahead like an impassable wall of glass, brick, and concrete. On the last rooftop, before being right downtown, we part ways and begin our search for the strange man and the zombies. Erik, Matt and Paul head off to make a wide circling search of the entire downtown core.

Richard and I make our way to the fire escape in the shadows of the towering buildings. Looking out over the edge, the alleyway looks empty and safe. We climb out onto the rusty fire escape and descend its shaky steps. We drop down to the dirty alley and walk cautiously right out onto Main Street.

We look up at the towering buildings. The sun glares bright off the immense glass windows and reflects the sunlight in a blinding display. *If we weren't in the midst of a zombie apocalypse, it would be a really nice day*, I think to myself.

Richard and I slowly cross the downtown street. It is no longer a bustling plaza full of people and executives. The businesses are all abandoned, and the roaming zombie hordes have left the city a filthy ghost town. We both get the frightening sensation we are being watched.

As we cross the main plaza, the eerie silence is broken by the sound of breaking glass. I look over and spy a familiar face in a store window, and I slowly walk closer to investigate.

"Evyn, what are you doing? The hotel is this way," Richard says.

My curiosity quickly turns to sadness. The closer I get to the figures in the window, the more overwhelmed I become. The truth enrages me, and I fall to my knees in tears and desperation. I cry out in sorrow and disbelief.

Richard rushes over to see what has happened.

From behind the shattered glass of the shop window, my parents stare out at me. I can clearly see the green skin, pale faces, red eyes, and nasty black rashes.I cry uncontrollably and I can not bring myself to admit what I am seeing.

This isn't real. I try to convince myself, as I rush over to help my parents, but Richard holds me back.

"There's nothing you can do, Evyn," Richard says as he pulls me away from the horrific scene.

"It's my mom and dad! Let me go! I've got to do something!" I cry out as tears run down my face.

"Come on, Evyn. We have to go. We have to find answers if we're going to help everyone," Richard says.

"Let me go!" I struggle against Richard and watch in horror as my parents stare back at me blankly.

"People are counting on us, Evyn. Come on!" Richard pulls me away. "There are people like Chloe and the kids at the hideout who need us."

I calm down and collect my emotions before we continue toward one of the largest buildings in the city. The Grand Hotel towers over most of the buildings surrounding it. The glamorous and elegant landmark takes up almost an entire city block.

Richard and I find it odd that there are no zombies—no sign of anyone or anything—near it. Neither of us can figure out what to make of the empty streets or the awkward silence. We cautiously approach the large building and look around for any sign of the zombie swarms.

A block away from the hotel, a lone zombie staggers out onto the street.

Richard and I both stand perfectly still, hoping the creature will take no notice and continue on its way.

"It's just one zombie," Richard whispers.

"You think we can get around him?" I ask.

"Yeah. Come on. We'll sneak along the opposite side of the street." Richard signals for me to follow him.

We duck down and stealthily make our way toward the zombie. Being as quiet as possible, we crouch behind abandoned cars, garbage cans, and bus stop benches. We make our way up the street until we are right next to the zombie.

Richard sneaks up and hides behind an abandoned car, but he accidentally kicks an empty pop can. The silence is broken as the can rolls out into the street.

The zombie twists its head toward the can, and Richard and I are both frozen in shock. The zombie turns its hideous gaze to us. We rise from our obviously useless hiding places, and the creature lets out a bloodcurdling moan.

The zombie cries out, gargling on its putrid black venom. It moves closer and begins to violently snap its jaw at us.

Suddenly, we hear moans everywhere. Zombies appear from all corners—out of buildings, out from alleyways, up the street, and out from behind us. The swarms have gathered.

"We've got to get out of here! Let's head for that open fire escape!" Richard points toward an alley.

"The hotel is right there. Let's make a run for it," I bravely say.

"No way, Evyn. We have to get to safety. We can come back to the hotel after we lose the zombies." Richard runs toward the fire escape.

"There's no time to argue. Just go. I'll be fine."

I run toward the hotel. The path ahead quickly fills with zombies.

Richard grabs a garbage can and tosses it toward the zombies, making as much noise as possible. He distracts the zombies just long enough to make an opening for me to run to the hotel. The zombies split up when they notice me rushing towards the hotel.

Richard runs for the fire escape, and a staggering pack of zombies also follows him. He starts his climb up the building just as the zombies reach for him. He kicks their extended green claws and safely makes it up onto the cold metal ladder of the fire escape, leaving the moaning beasts below.

CHAPTER 6

THE CAPTAIN

I burst into the Grand Hotel lobby and up through its lavish front staircase. I run through a set of doors and enter a large banquet hall. Elegant tables with fancy tablecloths, dinner settings, and nice cutlery fill every table in the room. *A fancy event had been canceled because of the zombies no doubt,* I think to myself.

I run through the elegant room, hearing the loud moans and clattering bangs of the zombies behind me. I run into a stairway and try to catch my breath, as I slam the door and lock it behind me. I then slowly look up hopelessly at the stairs that seem to rise endlessly in front of me.

Bang! Bang! Bang! The creatures are on the other side of the door, and I know it won't hold for long. Bounding up the stairs three at a time, my heart is pounding painfully and my legs weaken as I grip the railing with my sweaty palms.

The banging continues on the door below. It echoes up through the stairway, as though it was following me, and I try to climb faster. My legs become more exhausted with every step. All of a sudden the banging stops. I look down through the stairwell ... the zombies have gotten in.

A bloodthirsty cry echoes up the stairwell. Fighting the weakness in my burning legs, I continue upward. Finally at the top of the stairs, I swing open the penthouse doors and run down the hallway to the first door I can find.

I crash through the door, and collapse exhausted on the floor. Hoping there will be another escape route, my heart sinks into my belly as I look up and see the captain. I know this man is the cause of the sickness. He is the reason all the people I love have become mindless zombies. I want to lash out and strike this man dead, but I know there must be some kind of hope for everyone.

I sit there, facing the demon I had heard about from the boys at the hideout. All sorts of warnings and cautionary tales rush into my mind. But the warnings seem a bit far-fetched and are quickly dismissed. The captain looks very modest and smiles rather politely at me sitting there on the floor.

The captain's tanned skin is fair and clean-shaven, and he is dressed in a finely tailored suit. He wears a nice gold necklace and a shiny gold watch; their brilliant luster is blinding. The jewelry gleams and reflects the sunlight. The captain's voice is deep and has a thick French accent, making it hard for me to understand everything he says.

"My apologies, young sir. Who might you be?"

"I'm Evyn Hunter. Who are you? Are you the cause of all this? Are you the reason everyone is turning into zombies?"

"I believe there are some misunderstandings between us. An explanation perhaps is in order."

The captain has several servants by his side. Their eyes are glazed and dreary, and they stare off into nothing. Their clothes look tidy and clean, and their skin is clean but very pale and gray.

The captain signals for his zombie servants to leave the penthouse. He signals them to confront the ruthless enraged zombies in the stairway. The servants stagger out into the hallway and close the door behind them.

"Long ago, I saved a young man from death. He would have

passed on had I not blessed him with the immortal gift of life after death. But after years of being my apprentice, he grew angry and hateful toward me. He believed I had cursed him. He turned on me and ventured off on his own."

"So your apprentice is the cause of this horrible zombie infection?"

"For years, I sailed from town to town in search of my old first mate. Following the aftermath of destruction he always leaves behind, I have traveled the world over—always just a few steps behind him. I now find myself here, still pursuing him to no end. I feel responsible for my old apprentice's decisions." The captain takes a few steps and gathers his thoughts before continuing.

"After witnessing the outbreak at the hospital, I realized it was too late to contain the spread of his evil zombies. My few servants are no match for the army my apprentice has spawned here. I went to the museum to retrieve my stolen journal, but it was already gone. The zombies created by my old apprentice confronted me again. Not given the proper ritual, they will never learn how to live as undead immortals. The process to give life after death involves a very important step that I never wrote in my journal because the power was too great. I kept it secret. I kept it in my mind. These zombies were not given the gift of immortality. Instead, they have the curse of the zombie." The captain stops to listen to the scuffling and moaning in the hallway.

"I saw my old apprentice at the museum, but I was too late. He is overwhelmed with anger and vengeance, seeking power he has never been able to control. He went into hiding and set his army of zombies upon me. Normally, I can control all the undead, but he has somehow transferred his anger and rage into them. Now I fear the worst."

"What could be worse than what's already happened? The entire city is overrun! All my family, my friends—everyone is a zombie!" I selfishly question the captain.

"My old apprentice has always been arrogant and selfish, but over the years, I fear he has become more hateful and vengeful. He would like nothing more than to be rid of me, and he will stop at nothing until he has conquered the world. I'm not sure I can stop him by myself."

"We've got to do something. Can't you figure out how to stop him? How to cure all these people?"

"There is a cure. We must break his connection with the people he has infected."

"I will do whatever I can, but how do we break the connection?"

"We have to kill him. There is only one other way to break the connection. I have learned from my servants throughout the city that my apprentice is hiding in the old living quarters of the museum. I will send you on your way to confront him with some of my own servants. They will defend you and ward off any infectious zombies."

"You don't expect me to kill him do you? I can't do that," I say.

"Here. Take this. You'll need it to break the zombie curse." The Captain reaches into his pocket and hands me a small vial of red liquid.

"What is it?" I ask, examining the red liquid.

"It is the last of an old blood potion. It will break my connection with him, severing the bonds of immortality I have given my apprentice. I wanted to get him to drink it many years ago, but before I could get the chance, he turned on me. He stole it, along with my journal, and set off on his own. From that point on, he became like a ghost. Always on the lookout for me, I was never able to get close enough."

"And this will save everyone?"

The doors to the penthouse crash open, and a swarm of hideous zombies pushes through the captain's servants. The zombies fight to get into the apartment, but the servants keep the zombies at bay.

"Quickly, Evyn. You must go. Be very careful—and do not trust the apprentice. You've only got one chance to get him to drink the potion. Go now. We'll hold these zombies off."

Several of the captain's undead servants and I quietly exit the apartment. Looking up the hallway, we hear the ghoulish moans of zombies trying to get into the apartment. Their cries echo loudly as we run into the stairway on the far side of the building.

The servants are quiet. On the stairs, they almost seem normal. There are no snarls, moans, rashes, or evil grins. They seem confused and timid. They know they are not normal—and will probably never again be in control of themselves. They follow me like lost puppies.

On a nearby rooftop, Richard looks down to the group of people walking out onto the street. He has to look closely to make sure his eyes aren't fooling him. I exit the hotel with several of the captain's zombie servants by my side. Richard has no idea what's going on.

"Evyn?!" Richard calls down, checking to see if I am a zombie.

"It's all right! We have to go!" I shout back to him. "Come on down."

Richard comes down off the fire escape, and I explain what happened.

All the wretched zombies in the area lose interest, slowly back away, and wander off.

Richard, the captain's zombie servants and I, head off down the street toward the museum.

CHAPTER 7

THE APPRENTICE

The old museum was once a mansion, and it appears very distinguished compared to the modern buildings of the city. With the sun starting to set beyond the horizon, the museum resembles an old castle with stone, bricks, and large cathedral rooftops. The dusty windows are dark and ominous.

Richard and I, along with the zombie servants, approach the stone brick walkway that leads up to the massive wooden doors of the museum. The doors open with a loud, resounding creak, alerting anyone who might be hiding within the museum.

We enter quietly, and the shuffling servants follow closely behind. Richard and I shine our flashlights into the main room. Other than the museum exhibits, displays, classic furniture, and elegant tapestries, the large room is completely empty.

"We should split up to cover more ground." I suggest.

"Are you sure that's a good idea?" Richard responds.

"Just be careful, and if you see anything come back here."

We split up and explore the museum, leaving the captain's zombie servants in the main lobby.

We carefully search the empty museum for answers and the

captain's sinister apprentice. I try not to be shocked by the exhibits, the darkness, or shadows. I make my way through the gloomy building. After searching what I thought was the entire museum—and coming up with nothing—I round the last dark corner and I am startled by the sudden bright glare of a flashlight pointing at me. I let out a breath of relief when I see it is only Richard returning from his search.

"Geez. You scared me half to death!" I exclaim.

"This is useless," Richard says. "That apprentice guy is probably long gone by now."

"Go check on the zombie servants. I'll meet you out front in a few minutes—unless I find something."

"Why would you want to explore this place alone? I don't know what's creepier—this old museum or those zombie servants." Richard reluctantly walks out to the entrance of the museum to check on the servants.

I also begin to think this is a waste of time. There is no sign of the apprentice anywhere. And then I notice the glow of firelight coming from the top of an old set of stairs, almost completely hidden by darkness. I follow the light and make my way up the creaky stairs into the oldest part of the building.

Closed to guests of the museum, the dusty attic had been used as a living space by the original family. Seemingly untouched by time, torches line the walls, lighting the room in a twilight glow. A small fire burns in the fireplace, and the old floors and walls show signs of their age. The room is old and has been untouched by any renovations.

A sinister voice bellows out from the shadows. The dim firelight reveals the captain's apprentice. Sitting in an old large chair with his head down, hidden beneath a hood, the young man speaks in a low angry voice. "You should not have come here."

"Someone has to stop you."

"Who are you to stop me? What could you possibly know about me?"

"Why would you turn all these people into mindless zombies? They're just helpless people. What could possibly make you want to do something like this?"

"Don't try to pretend you know anything about me or what I've been through. How could you possibly understand what it's been like to live for hundreds of years and feel your creator lurking behind every corner, waiting to kill you? You can't begin to understand why I have done the things I've done." The apprentice stands and quickly approaches me; removing the hood from his head, he reveals himself.

The apprentice is not much older than me. Arrogant and impulsive, the apprentice is overwhelmed by rage and power. His temper is only equaled by his hatred for his old master. Long black hair hides his young face.

"I know it takes a selfish person to mess with innocent people's lives like this. Dealing in powerful magic you couldn't possibly comprehend, it's having an effect on you. The damage you're causing—"

"You've been talking to the captain."

"He told me he saved you a long time ago and has been trying to stop you."

"Save me from death? Yeah, right! I was forever cursed into servitude—and forced to follow the captain's every command without question for a hundred years. I became a slave to the good captain, always following his orders. I was forever connected to my creator. The gift of immortality has strings attached. I began to see the gift for the curse it really was. I was never able to venture off on my own, never allowed to be free. Not until I stole the journal and the power for myself."

I can see the torment in his eyes. The apprentice beckons for his zombie servants. Out from the darkness of hidden alcoves, the obedient ghoulish zombies skulk to his side.

The apprentice whispers silent commands to the zombies, and they become completely enraged. The zombies begin spewing black venom as they bark, snarl, and heave their chests. They moan, contort their heads, and head off through the museum.

"Did the captain tell you I'm crazy, impulsive, and incapable of grasping power such as this? Arrogant and selfish—"

"You left out stubborn and foolish."

"So you've been talking with the captain, have you? Maybe I'll just settle this my own way! I'll ruin you! I'll destroy this miserable city, your friends, your family, and the blasted captain once and for all for what he's done to me!"

I take my que and run from the attic.

The apprentice shouting behind me, "It will do you no good! You will all die! You will all become my slaves!"

Richard quickly hides from the vicious approaching zombies. Like wild ferocious animals, enraged zombies run through the main room of the museum. The captain's servants step forward and plant their feet in a protective and forceful way. They grimace fearlessly in the face of the enraged zombies as they collide.

The battle between zombies begins in a fierce and stumbling fight. The bloodthirsty slaves of the apprentice run at the captain's servants. The zombies lash out, swinging and snapping at one another. Claws scratch, bodies are tossed aside, black venom spews, and deathly cries echo throughout the corridors.

"Run! Richard, get out of here!" I shout from the banister as I hurry down the staircase.

Richard and I exit the museum as quickly as we can, narrowly avoiding the battling zombies. Out on the street, we realize something is very different. Something has changed. Zombies from throughout the city stir and become enraged. Angry moans and horrible cries bellow into the air from everywhere. The sound becomes overwhelming as sinister zombies begin appearing from out of nowhere, more than ever before.

We are quickly surrounded. In all directions, vicious zombies snarl and bark at us. Even more zombies continue to stagger out into the street.

"We've got to get back to the hideout. We have to warn everyone and keep them safe," Richard says.

Richard and I are frozen as a dark sea of undead creatures closes in on us. We snap out of our shock and make a break for it. We run toward an alleyway and climb the fire escape to safety.

The dimwitted zombies run after us. To Richards and my own disbelief, the zombies begin climbing up the fire escape.

The apprentice walks out of the museum and yells, "You can run, but you cannot hide! There is no escape!"

Back at the hideout, Chloe discovers the challenging task of keeping dozens of young kids occupied. Managing so many is much more challenging than she thought it would be. In the absence of the older boys, the hideout has become a madhouse. Without their stern and commanding methods of keeping the kids quiet, the children become restless and hyper.

Some of the children run all over the apartment, playfully chasing one another, laughing, and pretending to be zombies. Others make a mess in the kitchen, attempting to cook, or try to make unusual artwork from random food supplies.

With very little help from the older kids, Chloe tries hard not to explode. She attempts to calm everyone down without losing her temper.

Above all the noise, the young girl Marcy sits alone and quietly reads her favorite book. Suddenly, Marcy thinks she can hear something coming from downstairs. She gets up from her quiet spot in the living room and makes her way toward the stairway. She curiously listens to the muffled sounds of something scratching at the outer door of the building.

"Chloe? I think I hear something."

Chloe is trying to stop the kids from making a mess in the kitchen and cannot hear Marcy's quiet warning.

Marcy crawls through the barricaded doors and sneaks out into the hallway. The curious scratching sounds continue from below.

Rounding the corner of the hallway, Marcy investigates further. She sees shadows moving outside the front of the building. The scratching continues. As she gets closer, she looks from the safety of the banister at the top of the stairs. The front entrance is still locked and barricaded with wooden planks and cluttered furniture.

The curiosity is too much for the young girl. Marcy wants to see what's causing such an unusual noise. Her tiny footsteps fall cautiously and quietly as she inches her way closer to the front door. The scratching and soft thumps suddenly erupt with a horrifying moan, and a green claw smashes through a wooden board and reaches for Marcy.

She falls back onto the lobby floor and lets out a high-pitched scream. More shadowy figures appear outside, all rushing to gain access to the barricaded hideout. Marcy scampers to her feet and runs back to the hideout as fast as she can. "Zombies!" she cries out in terror.

"What are you talking about?" Chloe asks.

"Yeah. What's up, Marcy? We're safe here. There are no zombies getting in here," her twin brother Mike adds.

The hideout is thrown into a silent scare. Her cries distract the children from playing and laughing, and they all fear the worst. Everyone stops and listens carefully for any sounds of intruders trying to get in downstairs. They listen to the empty silence of the apartment.

"I swear they're downstairs trying to get in," Marcy says.

Everyone remains silent and listens more carefully. Suddenly, there is a loud shuffling upstairs. Heavy boots pound on the second floor, and the kids scream in terror.

Paul, Erik, and Matt quickly enter the hideout through the upstairs fire escape window.

"Where are Evyn and Richard?" Chloe asks, fearing the worst.

"We split up downtown. We thought they would be back before us," Erik says.

"We had to run. The zombies are on some kind of rampage," Paul adds.

"We don't have much time," Matt says.

Suddenly, like a raging thunderstorm, the bloodthirsty cries and clatter of the raging zombies come roaring up from downstairs; the menacing creatures have gotten inside the building. The hordes of zombies are on a rampage, and the hideout is under siege.

CHAPTER 8

ZOMBIE WAR

"**O**kay, everyone, hurry! Go hide in the bedrooms, lock the doors, and stay quiet. Don't make a sound—and don't come out for anything," Chloe says.

The horrible noises downstairs get louder, and more enraged zombies join in the assault. The hideout has solid brick walls and industrial doors, but no one ever expected this type of assault. The creatures terrorize the building like a rioting mob. They pile in through the building entrance, climbing over one another to gain access through the barricaded doorway. The swarm runs through the building—down into the lower levels and up toward the roof. Their sinister, contorted howls echo through the apartment.

With the front entrance locked and barricaded—and the large door sealed up tight—the kids believed they would not have to worry about the zombies getting in. Up until then, the zombies had been slow and relatively dumb. Not once have they behaved in such aggressive, determined ways.

The enraged zombies work together to pull open wooden planks that seal the doorways. They smash the reinforced glass windows and squeeze through them. The building quickly fills up with the ferocious creatures.

Richard and I drop onto an empty rooftop from the fire escape ladder. The horrid cries of zombies surround and overwhelm us with fear, and we take off running. The next building is only a short distance away, but the roof seems to stretch on forever. Before we can make it to the neighboring building, zombies climb onto the rooftop behind us.

"What's going on? They've never acted like this! Zombies can't climb—and they definitely don't run!" Richard says.

"It's the apprentice! He created all these zombies—and he's controlling them! He sent them on some kind of rampage. They're furious and following his orders!"

Before Richard can respond, more ferocious zombies come roaring and snarling out from every corner. Piling over the edges of the building, the zombies are coming from all angles. We run and jump onto the neighboring building, landing hard on the next roof.

The zombies run and jump in a feeble attempt to clear the gap between the buildings. Their uncoordinated legs are not designed for jumping such far distances, and the creatures crash into the alley below.

Richard and I feel no sympathy for the fallen zombies, and we continue to run toward the hideout. The growing army of unrelenting zombies furiously continues to chase us.

We are surrounded. The unbelievable odds are stacked against us, but Richard and I are determined. The rooftops all around us start filling up with the howling zombies and the streets below are even worse.

Like a raging river of tattered green monsters, the zombies swarm through the streets. They pile over cars, smash through windows and doors, and run up the streets. They scamper over themselves—forming mounds of disgusting creatures—and climb over one another while trying to crawl up the sides of buildings.

I peer out over the ledge and catch the worst glimpse of all. The sinister apprentice is just behind the sea of monsters, and he is walking along without a care in the world. He is actually enjoying himself as he leads his army of undead ghouls after me and Richard.

Richard and I run with all our might, our footsteps sound like crackling thunder on the gravel rooftops. The nightmare is amplified by thoughts of what could be happening at the hideout if the mad zombies have already made it there.

More moans and bloodcurdling cries come from behind us. Richard and I quickly slide down a fire escape. We clear the alley below and fly up to the next row of rooftops. More resounding cries of demented zombies torment us from the streets below. The zombies seem to be everywhere around us. The hideout is only a few blocks away, but it feels like it is on the other side of the world.

Richard and I are exhausted. We stop for just a moment to catch our breath in a sheltered corner on a rooftop.

"I think we lost them," I say hopefully, gasping for breath.

"Yeah right."

"We have to get to the hideout. We have to help everyone."

"It's safe there. It's barricaded and locked up tight. Everyone will be okay until we return."

We dart for the next ledge and leap to the neighboring building. In the fading light, we see the swarms of zombies and realize how monumental the evil army has become.

The rooftops behind us are filled with zombies. Crowds of them are trying to get ahead of one another in pursuit of me and Richard. Down in the streets and alleyways, zombies pile up, clawing and scampering on top of one another to climb up the building's sheer walls.

Neither of us can believe our eyes, and we try not to think of how hopeless our situation seems. All I can think of is all the people I care about as we run for our lives.

How horrible a fate these zombie creatures have? That same fate lies ahead for everyone not yet infected, I think to myself. *We must make it to the hideout safely, and help save everyone before it's too late.*

Richard and I hop to the next rooftop. Our feet land hard on the gravel roof, but we do not slow down. We run across the roof and on to the next one.

The sun is completely below the horizon. Darkness covers the sky and the ground, as thousands of rampaging zombies follow me and Richard throughout the city. Finally, we can see the hideout in the distance and quickly realize we are seriously running out of options.

The monsters continue to gather inside and out, the hideout is completely covered with zombies.

Chloe, Erik, Paul, and Matt start piling up all the couches and furniture to barricade the front door. The zombies have not yet found the loft apartment, but they are everywhere else in the building.

The lights in the room click off, and the apartment goes black. The young children in their rooms scream as the lights go out. The dim light of the moon brightens the apartment just enough for Chloe and the boys to see what they're doing.

"They've gotten to the generator," Paul says.

"They must have been attracted to its noise. Don't make a sound," Chloe says.

"Guys, what are we going to do? They'll be here any second, and I don't think we can hold them all off," Matt says.

"We've got to hold them off as best we can," Erik replies.

"What about the kids? And where are Evyn and Richard? We could sure use their help," Chloe adds.

To the dismay and horror of the kids in the apartment, contorted figures start appearing outside the upper windows. They were not expecting this at all. Panic sets in as the looming danger grows all around them.

The zombies have gathered in such huge swarms that they block out the moonlight as they climb up the outer walls of the building.

Chloe and the boys stand frozen in shock and horror as the darkness engulfs the hideout. They have no idea what to do next.

"Don't make any noise," Chloe whispers.

All of a sudden, in the silence and darkness of the apartment, the barricaded door lets out a loud and heavy thump.

The kids all jump in fright and turn to Chloe for guidance. She gathers her courage and looks around. All she can think of is how desperate their situation has become. What can they do against the horror awaiting them on the other side of that door? As strange thoughts begin to swirl in her horrified mind, Chloe calms down and tries to imagine what Evyn would do. She finally blurts out, "Grab something. Anything you can. We have to make a stand."

The kids grab anything they can find to defend themselves against the undead ghouls. They spread out and prepare for the onslaught.

Chloe grabs a kitchen chair, and Erik finds a kitchen stool. Paul and Matt take brooms and the ironing board from the nearby kitchen.

Another loud thump from behind the barricaded door startles everyone, and the dark figures outside the windows stop moving. The kids freeze in fear again. They quickly find the motivation and courage they need. Without any other option, they must defend the hideout.

Like an earthquake, the front door rumbles. The furious zombies violently bang away. The door cracks open, and the barricade opens a few inches. Several dirty claws reach inside. The wretched moaning outside the door erupts, and the windows crack and smash open across the apartment, as the zombies try to smash their way inside.

"Go! Block those windows!" Chloe shouts to the boys.

Chloe and Erik leap for the front door, pushing with all their might as devilish moans and whipping arms try to gain access to the hideout.

Matt and Paul run for the windows. With their weapons in hand, the boys shove the invading creatures down to the ground. The boys keep shoving the zombies as more climb up the side of the building.

The grueling battle continues inside the apartment. More infectious, green zombies join the assault. The entire building is full of the wretched creatures. Overflowing with blackened moans and deathly cries, the zombies rage on. They spew black venom and fight to gain entrance to the last healthy survivors.

Holding the front door at bay, Chloe swings the kitchen chair with determination. The constant barrage of blows keeps the zombies behind the barricaded doorway.

Erik tries with all his might to keep the furniture in place, pushing with all his might but the monsters keep trying to force their way inside.

Matt and Paul send a nonstop stream of snarling, black-mouthed zombies sailing down to the street. The zombies quickly begin to pile up, creating a mountain of bodies outside the building. Over and over, the creatures climb right back up to the window. They seem to grow in numbers with every swing. For every zombie the boys knock out the window, two more take its place.

As Chloe and the boys begin to lose their energy, they also begin to lose hope.

CHAPTER 9

FINAL CONFLICT

R ichard and I barely make it back to the hideout. With the entire town of Newport on top of us, the ravenous beasts close in all around. Richard and I jump fearlessly onto the rooftop of the hideout. We quickly get to our feet and realize it's too late. The hideout is overrun with zombies.

Huge droves of zombies have followed us here. We frantically shove the growling, bloodthirsty zombies off the fire escape sending them far down to the alley below. To our dismay, after smashing against the pavement, the zombies get right back up and begin climbing the building again.

More zombies join the swarm on the streets. Out from everywhere, they show up from neighboring buildings, out from alley ways and swarming from up the city streets. They completely surround the building with the hideout, all the kids, and Chloe.

The zombies continue climbing the building, climbing and piling up on top of one another to make it to the roof. The building is quickly covered; like an anthill swarming with insects, there seems to be no end to the zombies.

The ghouls climb over the ledge of the rooftop from all sides, clawing their way, and stumbling over one another. The moaning creatures sluggishly make their way onto the roof. Richard and I are surrounded, and there is no escape in sight.

To their surprise, the zombies begin giving up. The battle to save the hideout seems almost over, but it will be a short-lived victory.

Chloe and Erik hold the front the door closed as zombies try to bash and claw their way in.

Paul and Matt ward off the intruding creatures from the window, and there seem to be fewer zombies. Without realizing the onslaught on the hideout is far from over, the kids become overly confident. Paul and Matt lose focus for a moment.

A sudden surge of snarling, enraged zombies rushes the window. Four creatures burst through the window, knocking the boys back in a flurry.

Chloe and Erik experience a newfound terror at the front door. A zombie growls low and deep behind the door. The sinister growl sounds more horrifying than any other. After a moment of silence, the beast hits the barricade with such force.

Chloe and Erik get knocked hard and fly back several feet. The huge zombie hits again, and the barricade shifts open. A huge green arm reaches into the apartment.

Chloe gets to her feet and runs at it, shoving the furniture back into place, and swings at the zombie. "Guys!? I could use a little help over here!" Chloe turns to determine why no one is coming to help her, and she freezes in terror.

Paul and Matt have turned that sickly shade of green, their eyes are red and the gross rash has began growing up their faces. The boys stand there holding Erik helplessly on the ground.

Dozens of zombies pile in through the window. They make their way toward Chloe, and she backs away from the door, leaving it open to the intruding zombies.

Chloe's heart sinks, and she cannot breathe. Menacing coughs and black venom rain down on her from all sides. She hears the children whimpering upstairs, and she falls to the floor. Rage grows inside her body, a black rash grows on her arms and face as her skin fades to a pale green. Her eyes burn, and her vision turns a violent shade of red.

The vicious zombies stop, and the horde on the rooftop goes silent. Richard and I are completely surrounded and horrified by the army of zombies. As we prepare for one last stand—the final battle to save themselves and their friends—the zombies take a step back and separate.

The rampaging zombies quietly shuffle to the side, and the apprentice walks slowly through the ranks of his evil zombie army.

Richard lunges at him, but the swarm of zombies lashes out and grabs him. Holding him tightly, the zombies pull Richard to the ground, leaving him unable to fight back. With their menacing, contorted mouths, they cough black venom all over Richard, infecting him with the diabolical curse.

Looking at me with a sinister grin, the apprentice says, "You're next."

Richard coughs violently. He twists and turns in a contorted mess on the floor as the zombies back away. Richard eventually gets to his feet. He stops coughing, as a black rash grows up his arms and his face. A grin full of black teeth appears on his face. Just behind Richard, I can see my worst fear has come true.

My beautiful and loving girlfriend Chloe comes staggering up from behind Richard. My heart breaks a million times at once, more pain and sorrow than I have ever felt, beyond broken, my heart is gone. My head drops and I cry uncontrollably.

I can only look on through tear filled eyes in horror at the fate that lies just moments away for me. Her once beautiful skin and hair are green and grey, matted with dirt and grime. Her dazzling eyes are now red with rage and her smile that once mesmerizing and bright, is now filled with black venom and snarling jagged teeth.

I broke a promise. My Chloe is gone.

"Let me bless you with the gift of immortality, young Evyn—not the mindless curse of these zombies—but the gift of life in death."

Zombies take hold of me, pinning me into a helpless position on the dirty ground of the rooftop. I struggle with what strength I have left, but the enraged beasts firmly keep hold of me.

The apprentice claws a small slice into his own forearm and forces the open wound of black venomous blood toward my face. The drops of dark, black blood fall helplessly into my mouth.

From out of nowhere, the captain suddenly appears. Swift and determined, he grabs the apprentice from behind and holds him firmly.

The apprentice struggles to break free of the captain's hold on him. He bellows to his minions of undead servants to help him, but it's too late.

"Now Evyn! The vial!" The captain bellows at me.

I act quickly. As the zombies release me to help the apprentice, I can feel such an angry rage, more than I have ever felt before. Any sadness for Chloe, any reasoning at all quickly drowns out with uncotrolable anger. The overwhelming sensation of hatred begins to take over, but I fight it with all my might. I take the captain's vial out of my pocket. I yank the lid off, and in one motion, as my eyes burn and turn red, and the black rash sprouts up my face, I force the red liquid of the vial into the apprentice's mouth.

The apprentice is shocked, frozen in outrage, and completely petrified. His disbelief paralyzes him, and he stops struggling in the Captain's arms. He has lost his will to fight. The captain releases his old disciple as the apprentice collapses to his knees.

No longer bound by the captain's immortal blessing, the

apprentice begins to age rapidly. The hundreds of years he has been an immortal undead servant—all the years spent on earth—quickly begin to catch up to him. His black hair grows longer, turning shades of gray and then white, and his face starts to wrinkle and shrivel. The apprentice stares at his hands as they begin to prune like a hundred-year-old man. He calmly looks up at his old master and me. "I'm finally free."

Hundreds of years catch up with him. He dries up and cracks like an ancient statue. With a strong gust of wind, the apprentice crumbles to dust and blows away in a dark mist into the night sky.

All the mindless zombies—every one of the menacing, rampaging creatures surrounding the hideout and throughout the city—stop and stand still. The moaning goes silent, the black rashes and sinister grins fade away, and the green skin slowly turns back to a normal, healthy glow.

All the residents of Newport stand clueless, wondering what has happened. Their clothes and skin are covered in black and green stains, and they smell like garbage on the hottest days of summer.

They start their lonely walks back to their homes. Lining the streets, the curious people of Newport walk silently and undisturbed home through the dirty city.

CHAPTER 10

CONCLUSIONS

The sunrise casts its bright warm light into my room. The sounds of the radio fill my room as I slowly wake up to the DJ and soft music.

"The sun is shining, the birds are singing, and everything seems to be great out in the world, from here at the station with DJ Cool Boy. Newport Hospital reports that the illness that abruptly brought the city to a halt is nowhere to be found. Cleanup has already finished on the major streets, and officials state that everything is back to normal. So don't worry about catching any silly flu bug! Get out there and enjoy the beach, the mall, or whatever you want to do in our wonderful little city."

Still exhausted and unsure of what to expect, I turn off the radio and slowly make my way down to the kitchen.

"Good morning, son. You sure slept a lot today."

"Sorry, Mom. I was really tired." I am overjoyed to see my mom healthy again. Her rosy complexion and clean clothes are the most welcoming sight I have seen in days. "Where's dad?"

"He's in the living room—with a visitor for you."

In the living room, my dad says, "Good morning, son. A great new boss is here to see you. You never told me you got a new job, Evyn."

To my surprise, my dad is talking to the captain.

"I'm sure you two have lots to discuss about this new job. I'll leave you guys to it." My dad gives me a pat on the back as he leaves the living room.

"I have seen and accomplished many wonderful and mysterious things in all my years. I have traveled the world over many times, and I've rarely come across someone with such an uncanny ability as you, Evyn Hunter. You have a unique soul. It reminds me very much of my old apprentice when we first met so many years ago. He was different back then. I fear it was my fault that he changed."

"You can't blame yourself. You saved his life all those years ago. It still scares me to think of it, but I've got to ask, how old are you really?."

The captain smiles. "You are very brave, Evyn. Your courage and determination only seem equaled by your compassion and curiosity. Our meeting was not by chance. I've learned over the years not to believe in coincidence, and I feel our journey will cross paths again someday. I must leave now. I have a longing to return to my home and start anew. Take care, young Evyn Hunter. There is a bright, promising future ahead of you. Not much unlike a job you work at, if you do not stray from your ways, you will be very successful and your accomplishments will be many."

"But I've got so many questions for you. Can't you stay for a bit longer?"

"You have another visitor, Evyn. And I'm sure you will find all your answers soon enough."

I turn my attention to the sound of the doorbell ringing. I look back, but the Captain is gone.

Chloe walks into the living room and wraps her arms around me. "Who were you talking to?"

"It was the Captain," I respond.

"The captain of what?"

"I'm not sure."

"I'm so glad you managed to stop that horrible nightmare. What happened? The last thing I remember was fighting for my life in that old apartment. And the next thing, I was in my room."

"It all sort of worked itself out, I guess. I'll explain it all later."

"What's this?" Chloe points to an old leather-bound book on a chair. Right where the Captain was sitting.

"It's the Captain's journal. He must have left it for me."

"It looks like the book from the museum. Why would he leave it with you?"

"I'm not sure. But I think I'll find some answers in it. Come on. Let's go check on Sam. I want to see how he's doing." We head toward the door.

The sun is shining down over Newport. The perfect cool breeze from the ocean water pours over the town. It is one of the most beautiful days Newport has seen in along time.

Chloe and I head up Main Street toward Sam's house. The streets are busy with people. Shop owners are cleaning up, businesses are open, and people are enjoying themselves.

"Good afternoon. Nice day, isn't it?" Evyn asks the coffee shop owner.

"Yes, it is quite a beautiful day. Have a good one."

Chloe and I approach a teenager and two young kids with their mom.

"Evyn and Chloe!" Richard says.

"Hey, Evyn! Hey, Chloe!" Mike and Marcy run up and hug Chloe.

"It sure is nice running into you guys. How are you?" I ask.

"Much better, thanks to you. My little brother and sister really wanted to thank you guys for all your help—and for saving our mom."

"These two are your brother and sister?" Chloe asks as the young twins release her from a hug.

"We've got to get going, Richard. Lots to do today. It was nice to meet you both," Richard's mom says as she heads for her car.

"Can you believe no one seems to remember anything about the last week? It's like they all lost their memories after getting sick or something," Richard says as he corrals his little brother and sister into the car.

"It's probably for the best," I say.

"See you guys around," Chloe says.

Chloe and I continue on to Sam's house, but before we can even make it to his house, Sam comes running out as we are walking up to his house.

We are so happy to see our best friend in full health and smiling on such a beautiful day.

"Hey, guys! What did I miss?" Sam asks smiling.

Prepare yourself for the next exciting
adventures featuring Evyn Hunter

Coming Soon

Evyn Hunter Visits the Other Realm

and

Evyn Hunter Meets the Dark Prince

Printed in the United States
By Bookmasters